C000008253

Women and War
A One Act Play

by Jack Hilton Cunningham

A SAMUEL FRENCH ACTING EDITION

SAMUEL FRENCH

FOUNDED 1830

SAMUELFRENCH.COM

ISBN 978-0-87440-802-7   Printed in U.S.A.   #B2577

MUSIC USE NOTE

Licensees are solely responsible for obtaining formal written permission from copyright owners to use copyrighted music in the performance of this play and are strongly cautioned to do so. If no such permission is obtained by the licensee, then the licensee must use only original music that the licensee owns and controls. Licensees are solely responsible and liable for all music clearances and shall indemnify the copyright owners of the play and their licensing agent, Samuel French, Inc., against any costs, expenses, losses and liabilities arising from the use of music by licensees.

IMPORTANT BILLING AND CREDIT
REQUIREMENTS

All producers of *WOMEN and WAR: A ONE ACT PLAY must* give credit to the Author of the Play in all programs distributed in connection with performances of the Play, and in all instances in which the title of the Play appears for the purposes of advertising, publicizing or otherwise exploiting the Play and/or a production. The name of the Author *must* appear on a separate line on which no other name appears, immediately following the title and *must* appear in size of type not less than fifty percent of the size of the title type.

WOMEN and WAR: A ONE ACT PLAY was first produced by Owensboro High School and The Rose Curtain Players in Owensboro, KY in 2011. The performance was directed by Carolyn Greer, with sets by David Walker. The production stage manager was JoCarol Bunch. The cast was as follows:

BUDDY . . . . .John Thomas Priar/Jacob Chuter

HELEN. . . . . Helen Merritt

JACK . . . . Alex Priar/John Flaherty

BETSY . . . . Grae Greer

JOHNNY . . . . Isaac Settles

AGNES. . . . . Madison Stuart

VIETNAM NURSE . . . . Bayleigh Leach

VIETNAM MARINE . . . . Logan Sapp

DESERT STORM SOLDIER. . . . . .Alex Priar/Will Van Winkle

DOUGHNUT GALS. . . . . .Korin Cross & Chloe Tyler

WESTERN UNION GIRL. . . . . Grae Greer/Chloe Tyler

CHARACTERS

Casting for the numerous characters are at the discretion of the director/producer. Double casting, depending on available actors, may be desired.

BUDDY & HELEN – a couple in WWII

JACK & BETSY – a couple in the Vietnam War

JOHNNY & AGNES – a couple in the Korean Conflict War

In between the stories of these character's, there are a number of monologues; they are:

DESERT STORM CAPTAIN (HANK)

DOUGHNUT GALS (2)

SPECIALIST 4TH CLASS DELANEY

VIETNAM MARINE

VIETNAM NURSE

WESTERN UNION GIRL

AUTHOR'S NOTES

This one act is designed to be performed at, or under, 40 minutes. If performance time is not an issue, one or more monologues may be added to this script. The three additional character monologues are:

CAMP FOLLOWER
GOLD STAR MOTHER
HELLO GIRL

FOREWORD

When *WOMEN and WAR* began to come together and I married letters with monologues creating a kind of American war history lesson, the furthest thing from my mind—or expectations—was paring down the script to 40 minutes that would be appropriate for High School competitions. My original concept was to create a script that would be performed by professional companies, colleges and universities, and would be appropriate for young audiences from early teens to adulthood. It wasn't until I was contacted by Ms. Carolyn Greer, drama teacher and director at Owensboro High School in Kentucky, that I realized that my play's primary market was going to be high school productions. Teacher Greer asked if she might cut the script to fit into the 40-minute time restriction for her State's Thespian competition. I agreed. I put forth the stipulation that she provide me with her proposed cuts and I would do the same for her. We then compared our desired scripts and came up with this published script.

Reducing the script from 60-minutes running time to 40-minutes running time was no simple task. I insisted that the integrity of the 'history lesson'—if you will—be kept intact. Eliminating letters and monologues in their entirety would not do the job. Of course the first concern was which characters would be cut from the script. Several stand-alone monologues, like **Camp Follower** and **Hello Girl**, seemed to be the easiest to eliminate. The dueling **Mothers Of** ... and **Gold Star Mothers** would have to go as well.

Ms. Greer suggested that we split **Doughnut Gal** into two characters and that we add **Desert Storm Captain** to round out the script. Making these changes would allow for better casting and would allow for a more complete development of **Betsy's** character, making her not only Jack's widow, but also the mother of the Desert Storm soldier. I was reluctant at first but I trusted Ms. Greer's instinct, and in the final analysis she was right.

This exercise has been one of joy and satisfaction. Had it been with someone other than Ms. Greer, someone not as much in love with the original script, this process might not have been a success.

My thanks go to Ms. Greer. Also I would like to acknowledge the help and support given me by Amy Marsh and Katy DiSavino, both from Samuel French, Inc.

Jack Hilton Cunningham

Dedicated to

Carolyn Greer
and
The Rose Curtain Players
of
Owensboro High School

PROLOGUE

(As the house lights fade we hear the sound of radio static signifying the passage of time. The radio dial turns into various archival audio footage of broadcast reporting beginning with 9/11, various popular radio shows between the Vietnam, Korea, D-Day and WWI.)

(As the static fades we hear a recording of an instrumental WWII song like Glen Miller's String of Pearls. *Lights up on* **HELEN** *and* **BUDDY**. *The music fades under* **HELEN***'s first letter.)*

[The couples stand together, as **BUDDY** *discusses leaving, the couples say their goodbyes and the soldiers move about. All characters stay onstage throughout the show.]**

HELEN. Brooklyn, New York, April 1944.

BUDDY. Camp Polk, Louisiana, April 1944.

(Music out.)

HELEN. Darling Buddy,

Got your letter this morning. I was waiting on the stoop when the postman came. I can't seem to do much with my day until I see him coming down the block.

BUDDY. My Dearest Darling Helen,

I started this letter three days ago. I can't seem to put down on this piece of paper that we are shipping out...

(Sound cue: sounds of Helicopters then a song from the Vietnam era like Something's Happening Here.*)*

---

*Stage directions in brackets denote the staging by Owensboro's Rose Curtain Players.

VIETNAM MARINE. Danang, Vietnam, May 1967
Dear Ma,

Happy Mother's Day from your son. I've just arrived in Nam to the tune of chopper blades and the fireworks and blare of gunfire. It ain't no Fourth of July celebration, but have no fear, I have both feet on the ground and am surrounded by fellow marines – a great bunch of guys here from all over the states – even a few from good old Philly.

I promise to write as often as I can, but please don't expect too much from me. Ma, ya know I wasn't the best student when it came to writing and penmanship; so bear with me.

The chow here is OK, Ma, but I sure miss your lasagna.

Keep smiling, Ma; you'll always be my best girl.

[Insert Camp Follower *Part 1* here.]

(Sound cue: Jet planes.)

JACK. Vietnam, June 1968
Dear Betsy,

I'm writing this letter to say some things because in this flying business you never know when your next flight will be your last. Please don't think I am being morbid, but we all have to recognize what is happening here in Vietnam.

I want to be a comfort to you, but the distance separating us makes it very difficult for me to do so. All I can say is that you are in my thoughts during every sortie I fly.

BETSY. Chicago, June 1968
Dear Jack,

Your words make me cry. I see you in my teacup in the morning, and in the mirror as I get dressed, and in every young man I see on the street. I pick up your picture from my dresser and hold you in my arms. But Jack, I am *so* torn by the constant protests that are happening against this war – I know you are doing the right thing over there, but every night when I turn on the television news and I see men burning draft cards, and angry crowds shouting horrible things about our service men, I just don't know which way to turn. Help me to understand Jack.

JACK. Now baby, don't get yourself so upset. I know we are trying to do the right thing over here; all I need to hear is that you are with me in this conflicted, unpopular war. I think I'm strong enough to look past these times of uncertainty as well as to accept my mortality. If my plane does not return tomorrow, I will die without regrets.

(Sound cue: Helicopters or a song from the Korean Conflict era.)

JOHNNY. South Korea, May 1953

Dear Aggie,

The heat is unbearable here in Korea. Pork Chop Hill is no place to spend a warm Sunday afternoon, especially if you don't want to be shot at.

AGNES. Atlanta, May 1953

Dear Johnny,

Grandma Johnson is crazy about Johnny Junior. She thinks he's getting to look more and more like you all the time. Your mother insists that he takes after me more.

You would be so proud to see how good Junior is while we say the Rosary after supper.

JOHNNY. I used to dread those Sunday evening Rosaries when I was a boy. Knowing that fresh doughnuts and cold milk would be served afterwards, my impatience always caused some kind of disturbance. Gee, Johnny Junior seems to be following in his dad's footsteps.

*[Insert **Camp Follower Part 2** here.]*

(Sound cue: Radio static, a 911 announcement, perhaps a Rap song.)

SPECIALIST FOURTH CLASS DELANEY. I was seventeen when 9/11 happened. That morning the television in the living room was blaring reports of airplanes crashing into buildings in New York City.

I told my mom and dad that I was going to do my part to help see that this horrible thing never happened again to our country. So I joined my high school's ROTC. After graduating the following May, I joined the Army.

(Sound cue: radio static – 60's tune.)

[The men are seated in chairs and on stools, the women watch over them.]

[Insert Gold Star Mother *Part 1* here.]

VIETNAM NURSE. Ah, you bet'cha. (*She is from Minnesota.*)

I grew up in a large family in a small town south of the twin cities. My dream was to become a nurse, so after graduating high school I attended a nursing program at our junior college. Having many brothers kept us all busy looking out for each other; when one got the measles, we all got the measles; when one brought home the mumps, we all had the mumps. I guess that's why I became a nurse. Then, I became a Vietnam nurse.

My daddy, as I left home, took me in his arms and said, "I raised six kids, five of them boys. Now they are all men, and here I am sending my only little girl off to war." That was the first, and only time, I ever saw my daddy cry.

When I arrived in the war zone all I could hear was...

"Get down, GET DOWN!"

[Women grab her to safety.]

I lowered my head and ran as fast as I could – I was there – I was in it – I was a part of it, and it was, and is, a part of me.

[Spoken as the actor is pulled upstage by the other women. The actors moved about to represent the images of an O.R. The men lift their heads and look out.]

VIETNAM NURSE. *(cont.)* My first day in the O.R. I looked around at a room filled with rows of beds. Chaos – the smell – the smell, the yelling – nurses yelling, doctors yelling, G.I.'s yelling.

[The **VIETNAM NURSE** *moves about, bumped by the other women as she speaks.]*

A body was plopped down on a table in front of me – a boy no more than 18 years old – a bloody sheet over his abdomen and I was ordered to "prep" him – that meant clean his wounds, shave him, if necessary, and "Oh, yeah! While you are at it, remove his arm that's just hanging by a piece of loose skin."

When I received my orders to transfer back to the States, I got up, put on a fresh uniform, packed my bags and went over to the O.R. to say "goodbye." The ventilators were popping – it was hot and smelled of blood, yelling filled the air – it was exactly as it was the day I arrived.

[The **VIETNAM NURSE** *moves about, moves through the chaos created by the other women as she speaks.]*

Nothing had changed.

[The men lift their heads and then stand.]

(Sound cue: a song like If A Man Loves A Woman.*)*

BETSY. Chicago, July, 1968

Dear Jack:

Well, the boys are off in every direction these days. Hank is finally old enough to be a Cub Scout, Bruce is playing Little League, and Paul has taken an interest in girls. Paul got his drivers license yesterday, so now I have another reason to worry. My men; they will be the death of me yet!

JACK. Vietnam, August 1968

Betsy dear,

I have been thinking, if anything happens to me, don't let the memories of me keep you from marrying again. I just don't want you to be alone. Life should be lived to the fullest. Go for it girl – live life, that's what it is for.

BETSY. Now Jack, there is no need to talk like that. I believe that you will be resuming your fatherly and husbandly duties before long.

JACK. Keep on smiling, put on some makeup, buy yourself a new dress, give the boys a hug, some discipline when needed, and pave the road of your life for new adventures. As long as I'm remembered, I'll not really be dead. I'll still be around in Paul, Bruce, and Hank.

BETSY. Now Jack, you shouldn't go on and on like that. You *will* come home Jack, I know you will. I do plan on buying a new dress, and I'll have the boys all starched and ironed and standing at attention when you walk up that walk and into my arms.

The boys send their love,

Betsy

JACK. Love you Betsy,

Jack

[Insert Gold Star Mother *Part 2* here.]

(Sound Cue: a song like Boogie Woogie Bugle Boy.*)*

DOUGHNUT GALS. (*Note:* **DOUGHNUT GALS** *can be played by one or two actors.*)

ALICE. I know you've heard of the U.S.O. Girls who toured behind the lines to entertain the troops.

MOLLY. Well, we were Doughnut Gals, the gals that drove two-ton army trucks and served doughnuts…

ALICE. …and hot steaming coffee to the men.

MOLLY. Well, we called ourselves Doughnut Gals. Molly is my name. From down south, Alabama.

ALICE. I'm Alice from Cal-I-forn-I-A. (*Delete line if played by one actor.*)

MOLLY. Alice, my doughnut companion, and me…

ALICE. …ended up somewhere in France to serve our boys hot coffee and doughnuts.

MOLLY. So, me and Alice would load our old truck with sacks of flour, sugar and coffee…

ALICE. …and cans of cooking oil…

MOLLY. …and hit the road by five every morning.

ALICE & MOLLY. *What a bumpy ride!*

ALICE. Did you know that a greater percentage of Doughnut Gals were killed in action in the European Theater than gals from any of the other women's services?

MOLLY. *Put that in your record book, Uncle Sam!* In 1945 Alice and I split up…

ALICE. …I (Alice) was sent to Le Harve…

MOLLY. …and well lucky me, I was sent to England where my doughnut days continued and my jitterbugging days began.

[Actors partner up, with different time periods mingling. U.S.O. gals, flirting with the boys.]

There was this very large, empty warehouse building where the boys assembled for their next assignments. There was lots of music, and the boys loved to jitterbug, and since I knew a few steps – *move over English gals* – I went from being just a 'Doughnut Gal' to a 'jitterbug gal'. Give 'em some hot coffee and doughnuts, and jitter they would. And oh boy, could those boys jitterbug.

[A holiday tune plays, like Irving Berlin's White Christmas, *couples return to their original partner, forming a happy family image.* **HELEN** *walks past each couple as she listens to* **BUDDY***'s letter.]*

BUDDY. France, Christmas Eve, 1944

Helen, my darling,

My days are bluer than ever, and when I think of you, I have to fight back the tears so my buddies won't see. All of us guys left in Company B sit around in our dirty uniforms, heavy boots, and heavy hearts, and sing "Peace on Earth, Good Will to Men".

HELEN. Brooklyn, Christmas Day, 1944

Sweet, sweet Buddy,

Mr. Berlin hit it right this year. We don't have to dream; we have a white Christmas. I woke up this morning and looked outside to a glorious day. I was elated, but only for a moment, and then I prayed this will be the last Christmas we spend apart.

(Sound cue: a song like I'll Be Seeing You.*)*

HELEN. Buddy, I love you.

BUDDY. I love you, Helen.

BETSY. I love you, Jack.

JACK. I love you, Betsy.

AGNES. I love you, Johnny.

JOHNNY. I love you, Agnes.

[The couples walk upstage hand and hand, except for **JACK** *and* **BETSY**. **JACK** *walks away, leaving* **BETSY** *alone for a beat.]*

[Insert Hello Girl *Part 1* here.]

SPECIALIST FOURTH CLASS DELANEY. After my basic training I served a tour in Afghanistan in a non-combat situation. Women weren't allowed in combat roles, and still ain't. I was serving over there when my truck was hit. Three soldiers were killed and I was seriously wounded. When I woke up I discovered that my legs was so badly damaged that both of 'em had to be amputated just under the knees. I survived, as you can see, and with my prosthesis I can walk as normal as any of you here. Well, the downer is that I can't dance no more, can't wear skirts or dresses, just pants for me now – but that's cool – I can deal with that.

*[*DELANEY *turns upstage, all of the soldiers stand to pay their respects.]*

(Sound cue: a song like Near You.*)*

JOHNNY. Korea, April 1954

Dear Aggie and Little Johnny,

I can't explain why I have not been writing more. But you see, here in this mess, there is not a solider with a rifle that knows which way to point. We hear the enemy fire, we see the tracers light up the sky, and some times we are just lucky, like the other day when we captured those North Koreans.

AGNES. Atlanta, April 1954

Dear Johnny,

[She approaches JOHNNY, *runs her fingers through what used to be hair.]*

I let your mom and dad read your letter. You should have seen your dad's face when he read about the 28 prisoners you captured. That was something else for him to brag about.

You're so thoughtful, honey. That's one of the many, many things I love so much about you, Johnny darling. There isn't any more news so I'll close for now.

JOHNNY. This morning we encountered, face-to-face, a team of North Koreans. They were lobbing grenades and firing at us, and as they charged toward us I fired and hit one in the face. I watched as he fell silent and died almost instantly.

*[*AGNES *turns away, dropping her head. When he turns to see her, she is looking away.]*

Agnes, I can't tell you how awful I feel to have killed another man. I immediately asked God to forgive me, and I will go to confession the first chance I get. I am so confused. Oh, Agnes, please forgive me as well.

*[*AGNES *rises, looks at* JOHNNY, *and then calmly sits in his chair.]*

AGNES. We put little Johnny in Kindergarten this week. I do believe it was harder on me to leave him, than it was for him on the first day. He seems to be having a wonderful time with the other boys and girls and is learning his numbers and alphabet so fast.

Oh, Johnny, I pray that when this war is over there will be no more wars, so little Johnny and all the boys and girls can grow up in a world of peace and freedom. I know that day will come, Johnny, and I am doing my part to see that it does.

[He kneels by her chair and she rests her head on his shoulder.]

[Insert Hello Girl *Part 2* here.]

(Sound cue: a song like Long and Winding Road.*)*

BETSY. Chicago, September 1968

Dear Jack,

[JACK comes forward, standing just behind BETSY.]

It has been a week since your last letter. I hope and pray that you are just so busy flying sorties that you haven't had the time to write. Bruce had his first date last night; I dropped them off at Bloomfields for ice cream sodas, and finished my turn as chauffeur by driving Bruce's girl home. Bruce walked her to her door – you would have been proud.

[He places his arms on her shoulder, she does not feel his touch and steps out of his embrace.]

I guess our boys are growing up. Time for bed. I'll write again soon.

Betsy.

(Sound cue: a song like Wanted Dead or Alive.*)*

DESERT STORM CAPTAIN (HANK). Kuwait, February 25, 1991

Dear Mom,

There is sand everywhere – they are calling it Desert Storm. I'm OK Mom, but some of my buddies are dead.

Don't worry about me, Mom.

The news journalists and film crews are embedded with us now Mom. But I believe that they are not telling the truth to folks back home. Between the wind and the sand they seem to be looking through rose colored glasses. The horrors, the hardships, the total disbelief that we are living through this hell does not seem to impress them. So don't believe all you see on TV or read in the newspapers and magazines. We are in a living hell.

[He starts to walk away, **BETSY** *rises, approaches him and smooths the front of his jacket, just as she has done for his father* **JACK** *in an earlier scene.]*

We lost our first female soldier yesterday – she was only a supply officer, but still – Women and War!

(He turns, looks at **BETSY**, *and acknowledges for the first time that she is his mother.)*

I need some sleep, Mom. I send my best to my big brothers Bruce and Paul.

Love, Hank

(Sound cue: a song like Moonlight Serenade.*)*

BUDDY. Somewhere in France, January, 1945

Christmas and New Year's were just two more days for us. The weather is rotten. Wish I had some good news to send, Sweet Pea, but I don't.

HELEN. My Darling,

I got a job down at the navy yards; it's hard work, but I don't complain. Women all over this country are going to work and keeping house and being mothers and feeding their families even with the rations of sugar and butter. Last week there was no butter to be had so we bought oleo-margarine, it comes in a block, white as lard, with a little packet of yellow coloring that you mix with the oleo till it looks like butter. But it tastes like lard.

BUDDY. Sugar, you are sugar enough for me. Keep your head high and never lose that beautiful smile that I fell in love with. Don't worry about the butter, or me, I will butter you up when I get back to Brooklyn!

HELEN. I love you.

BUDDY. I love you.

(Sound cue: a song like Fortunate Son.*)*

VIETNAM MARINE. Tay Ninh Province, Nam, October, 1968
Little Brother,

(Sound out.)

Take this advice from me. Stay as far away as you can from the God forsaken army and this crap-hole called Nam. Trust me, being a grunt in this country ain't no fun. Don't be like me, go to college and get good grades or burn your draft card and head straight to Canada. Do this one thing for me, brother. And if I ever get home, I promise to be the big brother that I never was before. And, oh yeah, give Ma a big kiss for the both of us.

I never said this before, but I love you kid.

Your Big Brother

(Sound Cue: a mournful tune – piano.)

BETSY. *[JACK tries to approach* **BETSY** *but is unable. He stands at a distance, watching and responding.]*
Chicago, October, 1968
Dear Jack,

It has been three weeks now and no word from you. The boys and I are beginning to worry. Please just send a card to let us know that you are OK. Everything is good here. I bought that new dress today – this waiting is taking its toll on me, but I keep smiling.

(Sound cue: a song like Volcano Girls.*)*

SPECIALIST FOURTH CLASS DELANEY. I suffer from what they call post-traumatic stress disorder. When I started therapy it seemed to me that my symptoms was only caused because I lost my legs. I don't remember nothing – I might have passed out – I don't know – but I was the victim of a terrorist attack on my unit and three of my fellow soldiers was killed – two men and one woman.

Did you know that one out of every ten people serving in the armed forces today is a woman and I read somewhere that over 220,000 or 11 percent of troops sent to Afghanistan and Iraq were women? In the Vietnam War the percentage of women to men was much, much smaller and almost all of them women was nurses. Not so in today's army.

Now there's a large number of soldiers that don't think of the women as "sisters, wives or sweethearts."

[Another girl supports her as she prepares to speak.]

This ain't easy to talk about – well here it is, and I swear this on my Grandmama's grave – I was raped when I was in Afghanistan – by my first lieutenant. Because I was only an enlisted soldier, I was afraid that if I reported it, I wouldn't be believed. He was handsome, a very popular officer amongst the troops, so who would believe that I hadn't agreed to have sex with him? I ain't condemning all the men who serve their country honorably, but the percentage that takes advantage of their female counterparts is greater than the numbers say.

(Sound Cue: a song like Tuxedo Junction. *The sound vanishes and there is a beat or two of silence.)*

WESTERN UNION GIRL. Sometimes I come to the icebox, open the door, and just stand here, wondering what it was that I came here for. Memory is a funny thing at my age. "Madge McAlister," I say to myself, "what's come over you?" Then I hear the tick-tock-tick of the old regulator in the hall, and I am back one day in June, 1944.

WESTERN UNION GIRL. *(cont.)* After high school most of the boys of Baylor went right to work in the mills or on their family's farm; few if any, ever went to college. So for a few extra dollars they joined the National Guard and spent one night a month playing soldier. Aaron, my older brother, joined the Guard as soon as he was old enough. When the war began in Europe, his entire unit was called into active duty.

I worked as the Western Union Girl in Baylor, Kentucky and it was my job each morning to turn the Teletype machine on and connect with Lexington.

It was June 6, 1944 when our boys were sent to that beach in France the army called Omaha. Heroes all, over 10,000 lost their lives and were buried on the bluff overlooking the sea.

On that morning in June I switched on the Teletype machine, and when it warmed up I typed "Good Morning, Lexington, go ahead." And the reply came, "Good Morning Baylor. We have casualties." The machine began to sputter and click-click-click, shooting out tape faster than I had ever seen before.

Click-click-click, the tape just kept coming. *[from here, the clicks are said by the ensemble instead of the actor.]* I did my best to put the tape in the tank of water, and with my thimble and ruler stripped it onto the yellow Western Union stationary. *[The females will round robin the movements Madge makes as she explains the process.]* "The Secretary of War desires me to express my feeling of regret" – click-click-click. Another yellow piece of paper – another regret – another name – another address. I pasted and I pasted. Click-click-click – "regret" John Seers, click "regret" Albert Staulings, click "regret" Andy Barrow, click-click-click. "regrets" Bobby Barnes, "regrets" Dudley Dickerson, "regrets" Larry Holloway – click-click-click.

All in all, there were more telegrams than I can remember. As lunchtime approached I was pretty much in a daze and then...click-click-click..."It is with profound regret that I – click – Aaron MacAlister" – my dear brother...

(A beat of silence as she composes herself.)

In 1994 on the fiftieth anniversary of D-Day, I went to France and among the rows and rows of white marble crosses, on a bluff overlooking the sea, I found my beloved brother, Aaron.

[The company turns away from audience, and then turns back.]

Now, what was it that I came to the icebox for? Oh yeah, the milk.

(Another beat of silence and then a sound cue: a song like My Funny Valentine.*)*

AGNES. Johnny Jr. is so much like you Johnny, more and more each day, I see you in him. Even your mother is beginning to see you in the way he walks across the floor and turns and looks at us with those big brown eyes. She sings him a song that she said she used to sing to you. Do you remember it, Johnny? It goes something like this: "Oh, Johnny, Oh, Johnny, how you can love, Oh, Johnny, Oh, Johnny, heavens above."

JOHNNY. I used to get so embarrassed when she sang that song and my friends were there. But now that I think back, it was such an endearing thing that she did. I know she loved me more than anything. Since I was an only child, she had lots of love to give. Our little Johnny must have brothers and sisters. And I'll see to that when I get home. And Aggie, not to worry, but I took some serious shrapnel in my right thigh, but the medics tell me everything is going to be A-OK.

Love, Johnny

AGNES. Oh, Johnny, are you hurt bad? Johnny, I do worry. Promise me, Johnny, that you are A-OK and that I need not worry. *[She faces out.]*

I love you, Johnny.

(Sound cue: a song like California Dreaming.*)*

BETSY. Chicago, November,1968

Dear Jack,

They must be keeping you very busy my darling. Not a word in a very long time. I am holding up OK by propping myself against every doorway I attempt to go through. Not hearing from you is exhausting.

Mom and Dad are planning to visit for Thanksgiving. So I guess I will be cooking that turkey after all. There will be fresh baked rolls and pies coming out of the oven until we collapse from the sheer joy of cooking.

*[**JACK** turns away, picks up the duffle bag and slowly exits. The men acknowledge his death, while the women focus on **BETSY**.]*

Now that I have your mouth watering, I'll close for now – just wishing you could be with us for Thanksgiving.

[She looks for him…he is not there.]

Betsy.

HELEN. Brooklyn, April, 1945

Dear Buddy,

Not hearing from you is agonizing. The radio and newspapers tell us that the Germans are in retreat and that our Allied forces are advancing to end this terrible war. I pray every day that you are safe and will come home soon.

BUDDY. Germany, May, 1945

My dearest Helen,

I know you are worried since you haven't heard from me in months. As we crossed the border into Germany, we were ambushed and taken prisoner. We were not allowed to send or receive mail. Then our prayers were answered, and the allied forces arrived.

(Sound cue: a song like Wing and a Prayer *underscores the rest of this scene.)*

[Everyone celebrates. Congratulating one another, then a moment is taken, the **VIETNAM MARINE** *takes the* **VIETNAM NURSE** *into his arms and kisses her, posing in the famous kiss from the end of WWII.]*

HELEN. When will you be coming home Buddy? Now that it is over, over there.

BUDDY. I'm coming home Sweet Pea, hold your breath, I will be Brooklyn-bound on the USNS Buckner, a trusted old tub that will take me across the north Atlantic and into your arms.

[The actors form a tight circle around the **VIETNAM MARINE** *as* **BUDDY** *speaks.* **BUDDY** *exits. Music fades.]*

HELEN. Oh, my Buddy, I am checking the papers every day to see when the Buckner docks here in Brooklyn. I'll be wearing my prettiest dress and waving the good old Red, White, and Blue. Oh Buddy, you are coming home!

(Sound cue: Announcement of the end of the Vietnam War.)

VIETNAM MARINE. Boy, can my ma cook, she makes the best meatballs in all of Philadelphia. Ain't tasted that kinda cooking since I can't remember. Sometimes I just close my eyes and inhale, trying to remember those sweet smells.

Yesterday we went up the delta toward Cambodia. Our line of troops hit a snag. There was this gang of gooks waiting for us in the rice paddies. They eat a lot of rice here, not like us Italians – we eat spaghetti, macaroni, lasagna, and ravioli. (*He pauses briefly.*)

We were hit by enemy fire, and I saw my Sarge get hit – blood all over the place – he fell in front of me chokin' and spittin' blood. He died in my arms. The next thing I knew two of my buddies were hit. Private Lars Johnson was lying on his back with his blond curly hair all sticky with blood and mud, looking up at me with those big, blue Scandinavian eyes. A blank stare – another son dead – another Ma mourning.

VIETNAM MARINE. *(cont.)* All of a sudden there was the loudest explosion I have ever heard – inside my head – and all of the noises of war, the grenades, the copters overhead, the explosions, the shouts of pain and cries for help – all washed away into silence – sweet silence.

The fog cleared and everything was peaceful – just like eating your tiramisu, Ma – food I'll share with the angels.

(Sound cue: a song like Nearer My God To Thee.*)*

Ma, don't cry.

JOHNNY. San Francisco, August 1954

Dear Aggie,

Here I am again on the good old U.S. of A. soil – it feels so good under my foot. Yes, I said foot – the shrapnel lodged in my right thigh was more serious than I told you and my right leg was amputated. I hobble OK on one leg and one crutch. I'm sure Johnny Junior will have a field day teasing the "old man" as the "old gimp" now. I will get my final discharge papers tomorrow, honorable at that, and will be flying to Atlanta as soon as I can get out of here. It's going to be a new and different life, Aggie; so keep smiling, we are going to be just fine.

I love you and need you more than ever...

AGNES. Oh Johnny, Johnny Junior is jumping for joy and all I can do is sing: (*She sings*) *Oh* Johnny, Oh Johnny heavens above...

(Sound cue: a recording of Oh, Johnny.*)*

SPECIALIST FOURTH CLASS DELANEY. It's been ten years since 9/11. I am 28 years old, but I feel oh, so much older. *How did I get here?* Well, let me tell you – this is *my* story, but I am sure there are many, many *[women randomly sit]* more women with stories just like mine. We serve; we are abused; we come home – we fight the demons.

I may not be able to dance no more, not with these plastic legs, but that's cool, I can live with that. But will I ever be able to trust other men? Fall in love? Have a normal sex life, get married, and have children? Right now I ain't seein' that happening. I have heard of a program in California that is just for women who are diagnosed with PTSD (*She pauses.*), maybe I'll go there...

(*Sound cue: a song like* Black Bird.*)

BETSY. December, 1968. STOP Mom and Dad STOP The dreaded doorbell rang yesterday STOP Two young officers came to inform me that Jack is dead STOP At first they thought he was shot down and taken prisoner, but later learned that he had not survived STOP His body will arrive in California next week STOP I am holding up as well as one can expect STOP The boys are a great comfort to me STOP Please come STOP

Betsy.

[The women join her in saying the "stops" except for the first and last which she says alone. They build and then decline as they speak the stops. **BETSY** *exits.]*

(*Sound cue: a song like* In The Mood.*)

HELEN. Dear Friends,

My Buddy is home! (*Music begins to play.*) And you are all invited to celebrate the nuptials of Helen Sullivan and Buddy Brugaletta at St. Dominics Church on Flatbush Avenue in Brooklyn, on the 5th Day of October, 1945.

A reception will follow in the church hall.

(*Sound cue: an instrumental like* Unchained Melody.*)

[The entire cast returns to the stage, expect for **BETSY**. *The* **VIETNAM MARINE** *and* **JACK** *return, standing center stage and facing the audience.]*

WESTERN UNION GIRL. ...on the fiftieth anniversary of D-Day, I went to France and on a bluff, overlooking the sea, covered with rows upon rows of white crosses, I found my beloved brother, Aaron...

DESERT STORM SOLDIER. …We lost our first female soldier yesterday – Women and War!

SPECIALIST FOURTH CLASS DELANEY. …we serve; we are abused; we come home – we fight the demons …

[**BETSY** *returns, she is wearing a new dress.* **HANK** *stands just behind her. He touches her shoulder when she mentions the boys.*]

BETSY. …on the first snowy day in December Jack arrived home, his coffin draped in an American Flag. The boys and I met the train; I was wearing my new dress…

VIETNAM MARINE. …the fog cleared and everything was peaceful – just like eating your tiramisu, Ma – food I'll share with the angels – Ma, don't cry.

(Lights fade slowly after a beat of silence.)

ADDITIONAL MONOLOGUES

Playwrights Note: The following monologues may be inserted into the play, as indicated in the script, if producers/directors wish to lengthen the running time of the play. **Additional changes to the script must be approved by the playwright.**

CAMP FOLLOWER.

Part 1:

My name is Barbara Berry, my friends call me Babs, and I was a "camp follower." Now don't get your drawers in a twist – most people, when they hear the words "camp follower" immediately think of the girls who hung around army camps selling their company to homesick young men. I am not one of *those* kinda gals. Nope. I am a married woman.

After the president declared war on Germany, Barry, my husband, enlisted and was sent down to Louisiana for basic training, so I took the first bus out of Lawton, Oklahoma to join him.

Part 2:

Barry met my bus when I arrived in Alexandria, Louisiana. We needed a place for me to stay, so we found ourselves going from house-to-house, knocking on doors. After hours of, "Sorry buddy, but we don't have no spare rooms to rent," we passed a lady and her three young children sitting on a swing in her front yard. When Barry asked her if she had a room to rent, she said she only had four rooms in her house and no inside facilities except running water in the kitchen. But, she said, if that was all right with us, maybe she could put up a bed in the living room. She told us her husband was in the hospital and she needed money to pay the rent and feed the kids. Barry found an old davenport at a used furniture store not far from the house, and with the help of some of his army buddies, carried it down the gravel road to the little house.

CAMP FOLLOWER. *(cont.)* Later she moved herself into the back bedroom with her three children and rented her bedroom to another couple, Sally and Joe Malone from up north. Mrs. C, as I called her, also allowed us kitchen privileges.

One day Mrs. C told me that her landlord, Mr. Sweeny, gave her notice to vacate the house because she was running a house of ill repute. Well, he put it more bluntly she said, *quote* "You and yer kids gotta move, you ain't running no whore house on my property!" So she told me and Sally, "Gals, get your husbands and your marriage licenses ready, we are going to court." Ms. C couldn't afford a lawyer, so she pleaded her case herself, and won!

So we stayed and became known as Mrs. C's "camp followers." Now I tell you, Madam C was a saint to us, and no way was she any other kind of Madam. She took care of me and Sally, and other camp followers when we moved on, just like we were her own family.

GOLD STAR MOTHER.

Part 1:

I belong to the most honorable club in America. The Gold Star Mothers.

When a husband or son is in the war, a banner with a blue star is hung in the window. If a husband or son is wounded, a silver star is displayed. When a solider is killed in combat a Gold Star is given to the family to hang in the window so that folks everywhere would know the sacrifice that the family has made for our beloved country.

I proudly displayed three blue stars in the window of my modest house in Modesto. Folks would walk by and they stop there, some even salute. Passersby always ask if it was my husband, or sons. I stood proudly and I told them, "My three boys, Joshua, David, and my youngest, Adam."

GOLD STAR MOTHER. *(cont.)* Slowly my blue stars turned to gold. My baby Adam's star was the first to turn gold, and four weeks later, it was Joshua's. I wrote to my David to cheer him up and told him he is no longer the middle son...he is the only son. David's star turned gold before he received my letter.

Part 2:

I am a proud Jewish mother. Folks no longer stopped to congratulate me, but to console me. "Chin Up!", I told them. "What greater sacrifice can a mother make than to give her precious sons for her country?"

The gold star mothers have a heavy burden to bear. I stand behind our great president in these times of trials and tribulations. He gives me great strength.

My boys never left me...I still see them every day. Climbing that big tree in the back yard, scraping a knee while skating, chasing the cat and running after the dog, collecting cans and newspapers for the war effort. Before they left they started a victory garden and gave me strict instructions on how to keep it growing. Giving up a son is the hardest part of being a Mother... losing a son to war is the agony of motherhood. No more will I call up the stairs to them...no more will I sit up at night worrying when they come home late... no more will I fall fast asleep in peace when I hear the key in the door...no more...no more...

HELLO GIRL. *(She speaks with a slight French accent.)*

Part 1:

It was bitter cold the day when I landed in France in 1918 – a day that was much like many days in Bangor, Maine. I was an operator for the telephone company in Bangor when I heard that the Army was looking for switchboard operators who spoke French. I was one of 223 girls who would be shipped to France. We were sworn into the U.S. Army Signal Corps Telephone Units as soldiers. Think of that, the first women to serve in the Army and yet, at home we didn't have the right to vote.

HELLO GIRL. *(cont.)*

Part 2:

After arriving in France I was assigned to a station in Chaumont. The work was hard. Sometimes the noises of war made it difficult to hear voices from the other end of the line. We had to scream at the top of our lungs in order to be heard through the telephone lines – all the girls screaming into their instruments at the same time. I knew I was doing something important – the excitement – the constant noise kept me going.

I was sent from Chaumont to Souilly to reinforce the girls there. Conditions were awful. The weather was cold and it rained constantly. There was mud everywhere. The bottom of my skirt and my boots were caked with mud. The morning of November 11th, 1918 the hello girls handled heavier than usual voice traffic. Gradually the noises of war ceased. I remember that day well; it was another blustery cold day in November.

When the "hello girls" returned to the States we were told that we were no longer "sworn in" members of the Army. After failing to persuade Congress in 1930 to recognize us as full-fledged members of the military, more than fifty bills granting veteran status to the "hello girls" were introduced in Congress. Finally, in 1978 we succeeded. Congress passed a bill to recognize the 223 women as veterans. Only a handful of us were still alive.

OTHER TITLES AVAILABLE FROM SAMUEL FRENCH

WOMEN and WAR

Jack Hilton Cunningham

Drama / 1m, 4f / Bare Stage, Simple Set

Through correspondence and monologues, in the style of reader's theater, Women and War is a collection of fictional stories based on historical fact, told by generations of Americans impacted by conflict from The Great War to the War in Afghanistan. From housewife to worker, young bride to nurse, mother to widow, and now, young woman to soldier, these are tales of sacrifice, love, determination and hope told by those who bravely persevere on the home front and on the battlefield.

In Women and War, correspondence and monologues are used intermittently. The correspondence between characters places the audience in specific time frames and allows the audience a real sense of the relationships between characters. The characters are portrayed in their isolation, seeking an outlet for the expressions of their love and concern for their loved ones. Monologues are utilized to reveal what is truly going on in the mind of a character regarding the story they have to share. Correspondences and monologues are interwoven to create "through lines" of conflict, dramatic and situational irony.

While the individual stories are chronological, the entire play is not. For the purpose of comparison, suspense, and character development, lightheartedness is juxtaposed with the many obvious horrors of war. The element of relief has long been used as a theatrical convention in order to keep audiences entertained, while also addressing the need for a mental and emotional break from the severity of certain storylines.